Pooh's Pumpkin

Disney's
Winnie the Pooh First Readers

Be Quiet, Pooh!
Bounce, Tigger, Bounce
The Giving Bear
Happy Birthday, Eeyore!
Pooh's Christmas Gifts
Pooh's Fall Harvest
Pooh's Graduation
Pooh's Halloween Parade
Pooh's Leaf Pile
Pooh's Pumpkin
Pooh's Scavenger Hunt
Pooh's Sled Ride
Pooh and the Storm That Sparkled
Pooh's Surprise Basket
Rabbit Gets Lost
Tiggers Hate to Lose
World's Best Mama

A Winnie the Pooh First Reader

Pooh's Pumpkin

Isabel Gaines
Illustrated by Josie Yee

Random House · New York

Printed in the United States of America

Library of Congress number: 00-108704
ISBN: 0-7364-1142-9 (paperback)

First Random House Edition: January 2001

www.randomhouse.com/kids/disney
www.disneybooks.com

Pooh's Pumpkin

One sunny spring day
Pooh and Christopher Robin
saw Rabbit planting seeds
in his garden.

"Rabbit," asked Pooh,

"what are you planting?"

"Pumpkin seeds," said Rabbit.

"I would like to grow
a pumpkin, too," said Pooh.
"A growing pumpkin
needs special care," said Rabbit.

"I will take good care of it,"
promised Pooh.
Rabbit handed Pooh a seed.

Pooh and Christopher Robin
found a sunny spot
near Pooh's house
to plant the pumpkin seed.

"I will sit here
and watch the pumpkin grow,"
said Pooh.

"But Pooh,"
Christopher Robin said,
"the pumpkin will not be
ripe until next fall.
That's a lot of sitting!"

"My pumpkin
needs special care," said Pooh.
"And that's just what I will give it.
But first I have to get
something to eat."
Pooh went into his house
and gathered all of his honeypots.

Then he went back outside
and sat with his honey.
He watched the spot
where the seed was planted.
He watched and ate,
and ate and watched.
And spring turned into summer.

In the middle of the summer,
Piglet stopped by.
"What a pretty vine
you are growing, Pooh!"
he said.

"Oh, but Piglet,"
said Pooh sadly,
"I wanted a pumpkin,
not a vine."

17

Pooh went on caring for
the vine.
At the end of the summer,
a flower was on the vine.
Pooh was looking
at the flower
when Owl stopped by.

"Pooh, your flower
looks just right.
Keep up the good work,"
said Owl.
"Oh, but Owl," said Pooh sadly,
"I wanted a pumpkin,
not a flower!"

"Pooh, I will be happy
to tell you
what you are growing.
You have a vine.
You have a flower.

A flower grows on a vine
before there is a . . . cucumber!"

"You are growing a cucumber,"
Owl stated.

"Oh my," Pooh said.
"I wonder if cucumbers
taste good with honey?"

"Think, think," said Pooh
to himself.
"Rabbit gave me a pumpkin
seed. So it should grow
into a pumpkin.
I will keep caring for this plant
and see what grows."

Pooh went back to work,
watching the plant
and eating his honey.
From time to time
the ground seemed dry,
so he watered the plant.

One day the air was cooler.

The leaves were just beginning

to change colors.

Pooh had fallen asleep.

He woke up with a start.

Eeyore was standing over him.

"There is a green ball

on your vine," said Eeyore.

"Oh, Eeyore!" said Pooh sadly,

"I wanted a pumpkin,

not a cucumber,

and not a green ball."

"Oh, well," moaned Eeyore.
"I suppose we can find
something to do with it,
whatever it is."

Days and weeks passed.
The green ball
grew bigger and bigger.
Pooh's tummy was growing
bigger and bigger, too.

One morning Pooh saw
that a small part of the ball
had turned orange.
As the days went on, it became
more and more orange.

Then the air got cooler
and the leaves fell from the trees.
And on Pooh's vine was a huge
orange pumpkin!

Everyone gathered around Pooh
and his pumpkin.
They looked from Pooh
to the pumpkin
and from the pumpkin
back to Pooh.

"That pumpkin looks just like
your tummy, Pooh!"
laughed Tigger.
"Silly old bear," said
Christopher Robin.
"You gave the pumpkin
so much care
that you grew along with it!"

"Let's all carve the pumpkin
into a jack-o'-lantern,"
said Christopher Robin.
Owl carved the eyes.
Rabbit carved the nose.
Piglet carved the mouth.

Pooh's pumpkin was
the best jack-o'-lantern
in the Hundred-Acre Wood.